D0045231

Dear Parent:
Your child's love of reading starts here!

Every child learns to read in a different way and at his or her own speed. Some go back and forth between reading levels and read favorite books again and again. Others read through each level in order. You can help your young reader improve and become more confident by encouraging his or her own interests and abilities. From books your child reads with you to the first books he or she reads alone, there are I Can Read Books for every stage of reading:

SHARED READING
Basic language, word repetition, and whimsical illustrations, ideal for sharing with your emergent reader

BEGINNING READING
Short sentences, familiar words, and simple concepts for children eager to read on their own

READING WITH HELP
Engaging stories, longer sentences, and language play for developing readers

READING ALONE
Complex plots, challenging vocabulary, and high-interest topics for the independent reader

ADVANCED READING
Short paragraphs, chapters, and exciting themes for the perfect bridge to chapter books

I Can Read Books have introduced children to the joy of reading since 1957. Featuring award-winning authors and illustrators and a fabulous cast of beloved characters, I Can Read Books set the standard for beginning readers.

A lifetime of discovery begins with the magical words **"I Can Read!"**

Visit www.icanread.com for information
on enriching your child's reading experience.

I Can Read Book® is a trademark of HarperCollins Publishers.

The Angry Birds™ Movie: Too Many Pigs
Based on the screenplay written by Jon Vitti
© 2016 Rovio Animation Ltd., Angry Birds, and all related properties, titles, logos, and characters are trademarks of Rovio Entertainment Ltd. and Rovio Animation Ltd. and are used with permission.
All rights reserved. Printed in the United States of America. No part of this book may be used or reproduced in any manner whatsoever without written permission except in the case of brief quotations embodied in critical articles and reviews. For information address HarperCollins Children's Books, a division of HarperCollins Publishers, 195 Broadway, New York, NY 10007.
www.icanread.com

Library of Congress Control Number: 2015954426
ISBN 978-0-06-245334-1

Book design by Victor Joseph Ochoa

16 17 18 19 20   PC/WOR   10 9 8 7 6 5 4 3 2   ❖   First Edition

I Can Read!

READING 2 WITH HELP

THE ANGRY BIRDS™ MOVIE
TOO MANY PIGS

Adapted by Chris Cerasi

HARPER
An Imprint of HarperCollinsPublishers

Bird Island was a happy place.

Most of the birds lived

in Bird Village.

Some birds lived

outside the village.

One fussy bird lived alone

on the beach.

His name was Red.

He was angry

all the time.

One day

a strange ship appeared.

The birds gathered

on the beach.

They wanted to meet

whoever was on the ship.

They were excited.

They were nervous, too.

Two green figures

came down from the ship.

"Greetings from the world of pigs,"

said the larger pig.

He was round and had a beard.

His name was Leonard.

The smaller pig was Ross.

They were the only pigs

on the big ship.

Leonard and Ross

wanted to be friends with the birds.

The birds greeted the pigs

with open wings.

Everyone except Red cheered.

He was angry.

The ship's anchor

had been dropped on his hut.

No one cared.

That night

the birds threw a big party.

Red sat with his friends

Chuck and Bomb.

Red was still angry.

Some birds
performed onstage.
Stella led the way.
They shook their feathers
and danced to the music.

Then the pigs took the stage.

Leonard had a surprise.

The pigs jumped and twirled.

They bounced up and down.

Everyone but Red clapped.

He was too busy counting pigs.
"Weren't there only two pigs
on the ship?" he muttered.
The other birds did not notice.

The pigs had one more surprise
for the birds.
It was a big slingshot.
They called Red to the stage.

The pigs tested
the slingshot . . . on Red!
Everyone cheered
as Red flew away.

Red landed on some rocks.
He was back on the beach
next to the pigs' ship.

Chuck and Bomb found Red.

The three friends had a plan.

They climbed onto the ship.

Chuck and Red

found a closet filled with

crazy cowboy outfits.

Bomb was busy

bouncing around.

He hit the ceiling.

Then Bomb fell
through the floor.
He found the biggest surprise
of all—
more pigs!
Something fishy
was going on.
Red knew it.

Red marched the pigs
to the village.
They headed straight
for the party.
Everything stopped suddenly.
Red showed the pigs
to the birds.
He told them about
the crazy clothes.

Leonard had an excuse

for everything.

He said he wanted to make sure

the birds were friendly.

He was protecting the other pigs.

The pigs were going

to put on a cowboy show

for the birds.

The birds were angry . . . at Red!

He was told

to leave the pigs alone.

Red knew Leonard was lying.

The cowboy show began.

So Red left the party.

Over the next few days,

Red could not keep away

from the pigs.

They were everywhere.

They were on the streets.

They were at the diner.

They were even at Red's hut!

When Red spotted a second ship,

he was angrier than ever.

There were *too many pigs*

on his island!

One way or another,

Red would solve

the pig problem.

31901060720325